DISNEY · PIXAR

TOY STORY 2

ADVANCE PUBLISHERS

Published by Advance Publishers, L.C.
Maitland, FL 32751 USA
www.advancepublishers.com
Produced by Judy O Productions, Inc.
Designed by SunDried Penguin
© 2006 Disney Enterprises, Inc./Pixar Animation Studios
Original Toy Story Elements © Disney Enterprises, Inc. All rights reserved.
Toy Story 2
Printed in the United States of America

One day, Andy went away to cowboy camp without Woody! Woody's arm had been torn and Andy's mom put him on a high shelf with Wheezy the penguin.

Andy's mom wanted to sell Wheezy at her garage sale. Woody and Buster went to rescue him but Woody was stolen by Al, the owner of Al's Toy Barn. He wanted to sell Woody to a museum in Japan for a lot of money.

In Al's apartment, Woody met Bullseye the horse, Jessie the cowgirl and the Prospector. Woody found out he'd been the star of a TV show called Woody's Roundup.

Woody missed Andy but Jessie told him that Andy would outgrow him, just like her owner had.

Andy's toys saw Al on a TV ad and they set out to rescue Woody. After a long trip, the toys used traffic cones to cross a busy street and get to Al's Toy Barn – causing chaos on the way!

Buzz and the toys finally reached Al's Toy Barn and split up to look for Woody. Buzz discovered a big shelf of Buzz Lightyear toys. One of them grabbed him and put him in a box.

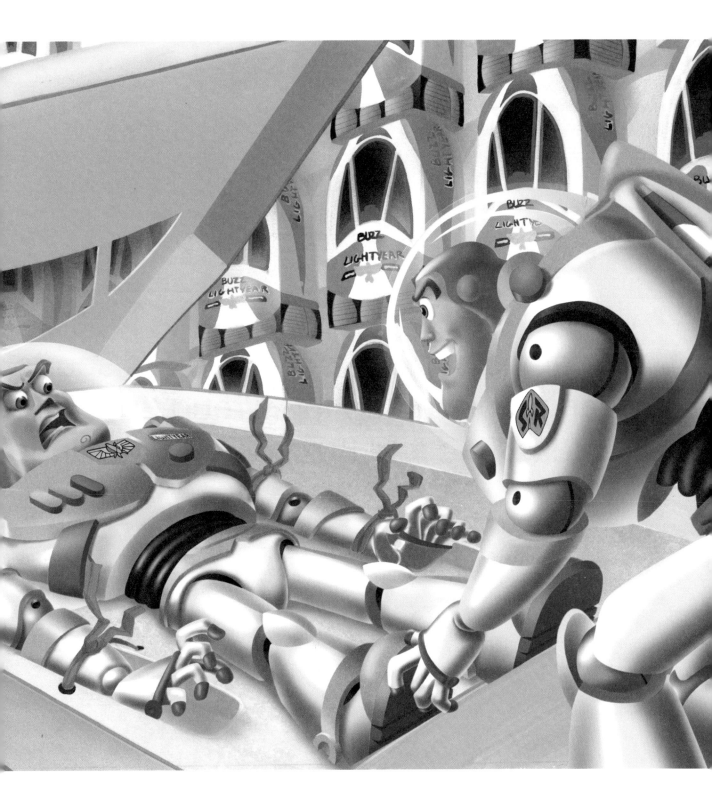

The other toys arrived in Barbie's sports car but picked up the wrong Buzz by mistake. The real Buzz was left behind!

With New Buzz leading the way, the toys found Woody in Al's apartment – but he didn't want to leave! "I belong in a museum," he said. The real Buzz finally arrived and tried to convince Woody to come home. But Woody wouldn't leave.

After Woody's friends left, he realized he'd made a mistake. But as he left to catch up with Buzz and the others, the Prospector stopped him. Al put the Roundup toys in a case and took them to the airport to send to the museum in Japan.

Buzz and the other toys followed him to the airport and into the baggage area. Buzz fought with the Prospector while Bullseye escaped. But when Woody tried to save Jessie, they ended up being loaded on the plane.

Woody and Jessie made their way to the escape hatch. Just as the plane started to move, Buzz and Bullseye galloped to the rescue!

The toys made it home just before Andy returned from cowboy camp. He rushed to find Woody and when he saw Jessie and Bullseye, he cried, "New toys! Thanks, mom!"

The End